12,259

J
K

Kaye, Geraldine
    Where is Fred?   Illustrated by Mike Cole.
Chicago, Childrens Press, [1977]
    24p.

    1.Christmas stories. I.Cole,Michael.
II.Title.

Where is Fred?

Geraldine Kaye

Illustrated by Mike Cole

Ⓟ CHILDRENS PRESS, CHICAGO

Library of Congress Cataloging in Publication Data

Kaye, Geraldine
  Where Is Fred?

    SUMMARY: A group of children go Christmas
caroling and lose the youngest member of their group.
  [1. Christmas stories] I. Cole, Michael.
II. Title.
PZ7.K212WH   [E]   76-51273
ISBN 0-516-03598-3

American edition published 1977 by
Regensteiner Publishing Enterprises, Inc.
All rights reserved. Printed in the U.S.A.
Published simultaneously in Canada.

Text copyright © 1976 Geraldine Kaye
Illustrations copyright © 1976 Hodder & Stoughton Limited.
First published in 1976 by Knight Books and
Hodder & Stoughton Children's Books, Salisbury Road, Leicester.

One night I was watching TV with Joe and Spot and Fred. My name is Jane and Joe is my brother. Fred is my brother, too. Spot is my dog.

Bang-bang on the TV.
"They got him," said Joe.
"I'm dead," said Fred.
Bang-bang on the front door.
"You go," said Joe.

At the front door Lynn and Tim
were singing *Away in a Manger*.

"We're going caroling," Lynn said.
"Want to come?"

"Oh yes," I said. "Can we, Mom?"
"And me?" said Joe.
"And me?" said Fred.
"Not Fred," Lynn said. "Fred's much too small. And he can't sing."

"I can sing," said Fred.

"He can sing," I said. "Fred can sing *Away in a Manger*."

"Only the first verse," Lynn said.

"It's dark and cold," said Mom.
"Look after Fred. Hold his hand."

We went to the house next door. It was dark and cold. We sang *Away in a Manger*.

Mrs. Jones gave us four pennies.

"A penny each," Tim said.

"What about Fred?" I said.

We went to a house up the street. We sang *Silent Night* and *The Holly and the Ivy*.

Fred sang *Away in a Manger*.

"He's spoiling it," said Lynn.

"Let's go to that house," I said.

"There's a big dog." Tim said.

"Spot eats a lot," Joe said. "He's a little dog. A big dog must eat a lot more."

We looked through the gate. There was a path and a window with long curtains and a Christmas tree with red balloons. Fred likes red balloons.

We went down the path. We went to the window.

"Let's sing *Away in a Manger*," I said.

Inside the big dog barked and the house shook.

A man came to the window. He
stood there looking out and we
stood there looking in. He shut the
curtains and then it was black
outside.

Quick! I grabbed Fred's hand
and ran. We all ran back to the
lamp post. Bang-bang went the
gate.

Under the lamp post I saw Lynn.
I had hold of Lynn's hand.
"Where's Fred?" I said.

I heard the dog. I heard the door. I ran back. Bang-bang went the gate as we all ran back. Fred had gone.

"Where's Fred?" I said.

Bang-bang inside the house.

Bang-bang very loud.

"They got Fred," I said.

I banged at the door and
the dog barked.

"A big dog eats a lot," Tim
said.

"He can't have Fred," I
said.

"Listen," said Joe.

I heard Fred. He was standing on a chair singing *Away in a Manger.*

"Isn't he sweet?" the lady said. "Have
a toffee, dear, and a cracker and a red
balloon?"

"Merry Christmas," said Fred.

Bang-bang at the front door.

"What do you want?" the lady said.

"Our Fred," I said.

"I've got a red balloon," said Fred.

"We're singing carols," Lynn said.
"Shall we sing *Silent Night?*"

"No, thanks," the lady said. "We've
just had *Away in a Manger.* First verse."

"Merry Christmas," Fred said.

"Sweet little Fred," the lady said,
as the door shut.

"We heard a bang," Joe said.

"Chestnuts," said Fred.